MR. TICKLE

by Roger Hargreaves

PSS!

PRICE STERN SLOAN

An Imprint of Penguin Group (USA) Inc.

It was a warm, sunny morning.

In his small house on the other side of the forest, Mr. Tickle was asleep.

You didn't know that there was such a thing as a Tickle, did you?

Well, there is!

Tickles are small and round and they have arms that stretch and stretch and stretch.

Extraordinary long arms!

Mr. Tickle was fast asleep. He was having a dream.

It must have been a very funny dream because it made him laugh out loud, and that woke him up.

He sat up in bed, stretched his extraordinary long arms, and yawned an enormous yawn.

Mr. Tickle felt hungry, so do you know what he did?

He reached out one of his extraordinary long arms, opened the bedroom door, reached down the stairs, opened the kitchen door, reached into the kitchen cupboard, opened the cookie jar, took out a cookie, brought it back upstairs, in through the bedroom door, and back to his bed.

As you can see, it's very useful indeed having arms as long as Mr. Tickle's.

Mr. Tickle munched his cookie. He looked out of the window.

"Today looks very much like a tickling day," he thought to himself.

So, later that morning, after Mr. Tickle had made his bed and cooked his breakfast, he set off through the forest.

As he walked along, he kept his eyes very wide open, looking for somebody to tickle.

Looking for anybody to tickle!

Eventually Mr. Tickle came to a school.

There was nobody around, so, reaching his extraordinary long arms up to a high window ledge, Mr. Tickle pulled himself up and peeked in through the open window.

Inside he could see a classroom.

There were children sitting at their desks, and a teacher writing on the blackboard.

Mr. Tickle waited a minute and then reached in through the window.

Mr. Tickle's extraordinary long arm went right up to the teacher, paused, and then—tickled!

The teacher jumped in the air and turned around very quickly to see who was there.

But there was nobody there!

Mr. Tickle grinned a mischievous grin.

He waited another minute, and then tickled the teacher again.

This time he kept tickling until the teacher was laughing and saying, "Stop it! Stop it!" over and over again.

All the children were laughing, too, at such a funny sight.

There was a terrible pandemonium.

Eventually, Mr. Tickle thought that he had had enough fun, so he gave the teacher one more tickle for luck, and then very quietly brought his arm back through the open window.

Chuckling to himself, he jumped down from the window, leaving the poor teacher to explain what it was all about.

Which, of course, he couldn't.

Then Mr. Tickle went to town.

And what a day Mr. Tickle had.

He tickled the policeman on traffic duty in the middle of town.

It caused an enormous traffic jam.

He tickled the greengrocer just as he was piling apples neatly in his shop window.

The greengrocer fell over backward, and the apples rolled all over the shop.

At the railroad station, the guard was about to wave his flag for the train to leave.

As he lifted his arm in the air, Mr. Tickle tickled him.

And every time he tried to wave his flag, Mr. Tickle tickled him until the train was ten minutes late leaving the station and all the passengers were furious.

That day Mr. Tickle tickled everybody.

He tickled the doctor.

He tickled the butcher.

He even tickled old Mr. Stamp, the postman, who dropped all his letters into a puddle.

Then Mr. Tickle went home.

Sitting in his armchair in his small house on the other side of the forest, he laughed and laughed every time he thought about all the people he had tickled.

So, if you are in any way ticklish, beware of Mr. Tickle and those extraordinary long arms of his.

Just think. Perhaps he's somewhere around at this very moment while you're reading this book.

Perhaps that extraordinary long arm of his is already creeping up to the door of this room.

Perhaps it's opening the door now and coming into the room.

Perhaps, before you know what is happening, you will be really and truly . . .

. . . tickled!

ISBN 978-0-8431-9896-6   10 9 8 7 6 5 4 3 2

MR. MEN   **LITTLE MISS**

PRICE STERN SLOAN

Mr. Tickle	Mr. Greedy	Mr. Happy	Mr. Nosey	Mr. Sneeze	Mr. Bump	Mr. Snow	Mr. Messy
Mr. Topsy-Turvy	Mr. Silly	Mr. Uppity	Mr. Small	Mr. Daydream	Mr. Forgetful	Mr. Nervous	Mr. Noisy
Mr. Lazy	Mr. Funny	Mr. Stingy	Mr. Chatterbox	Mr. Fussy	Mr. Bounce	Mr. Muddle	Mr. Dizzy
Mr. Impossible	Mr. Strong	Mr. Grumpy	Mr. Clumsy	Mr. Quiet	Mr. Rush	Mr. Tall	Mr. Worry
Mr. Nonsense	Mr. Wrong	Mr. Skinny	Mr. Mischief	Mr. Clever	Mr. Busy	Mr. Slow	Mr. Brave
Mr. Grumble	Mr. Perfect	Mr. Cheerful	Mr. Cool	Mr. Rude	Mr. Good		

$4.99 US
($5.99 CAN)

PSS!
PRICE STERN SLOAN
www.penguin.com/youngreaders

ISBN 978-0-8431-9896-6

EAN

9 780843 198966

5 0499>

DBK002099